Arrangements of syllabus repertoire
for lessons, practice and performance

Two violins

Book 1
Upper part Initial–Grade 2 standard

Published by
Trinity College London Press Ltd
trinitycollege.com

Registered in England
Company no. 09726123

© Copyright 2020 Trinity College London Press Ltd
First impression, April 2020

**Unauthorised photocopying is illegal**
No part of this publication may be copied or reproduced in any
form or by any means without the prior permission of the publisher.

Printed in England by Caligraving Ltd

# Sword Dance

Thoinot Arbeau (1520-1595)
*arr.* K & D Blackwell

# Fanfare

Michel Corrette (1707-1795)
*arr.* Mainwaring

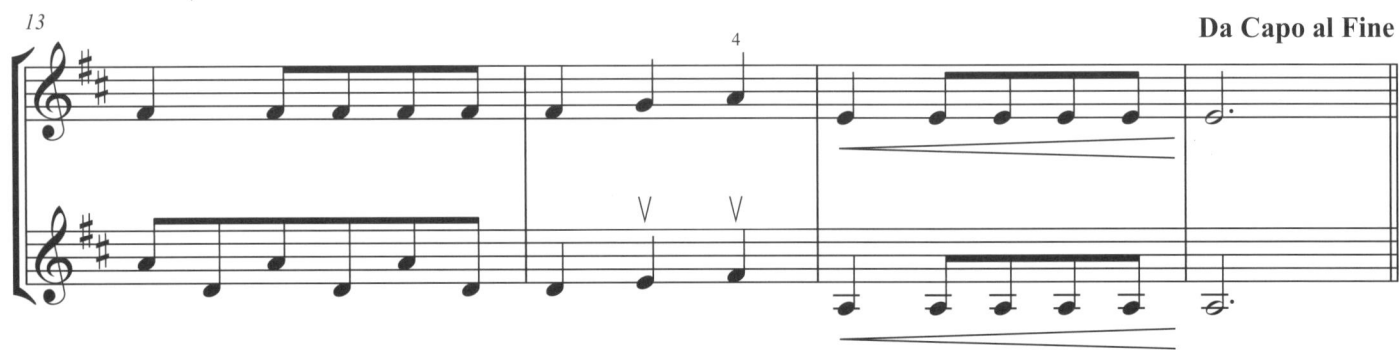

# Bell-ringers

Katherine & Hugh Colledge (b. 1952, b. 1945)
*arr.* Mainwaring

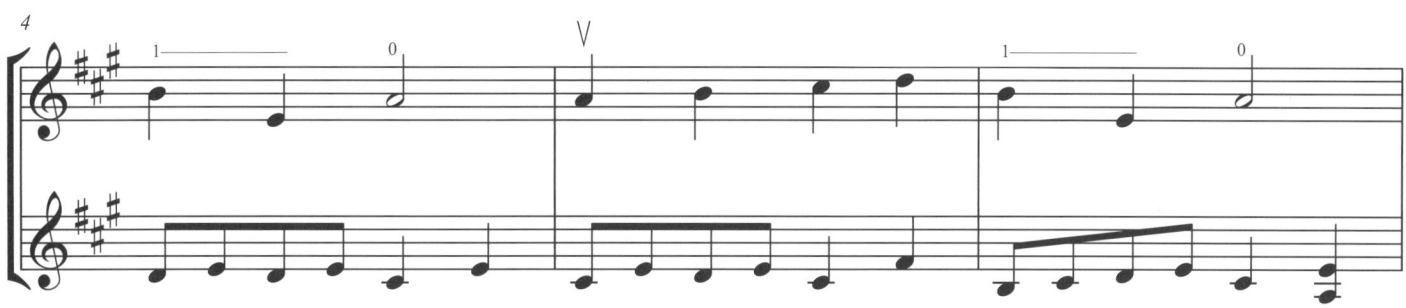

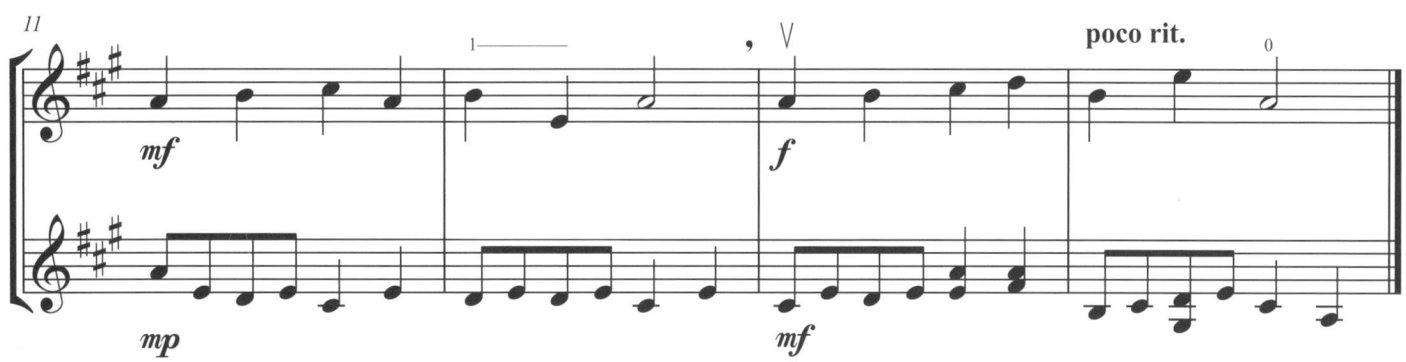

© Copyright 1988 by Boosey & Hawkes Music Publishers Ltd
From *Waggon Wheels for Violin* (ISMN 979-0-060-13553-8 & 979-0-060-13422-7)

# Knickerbocker Glory

Katherine & Hugh Colledge (b. 1952, b. 1945)
*arr.* Mainwaring

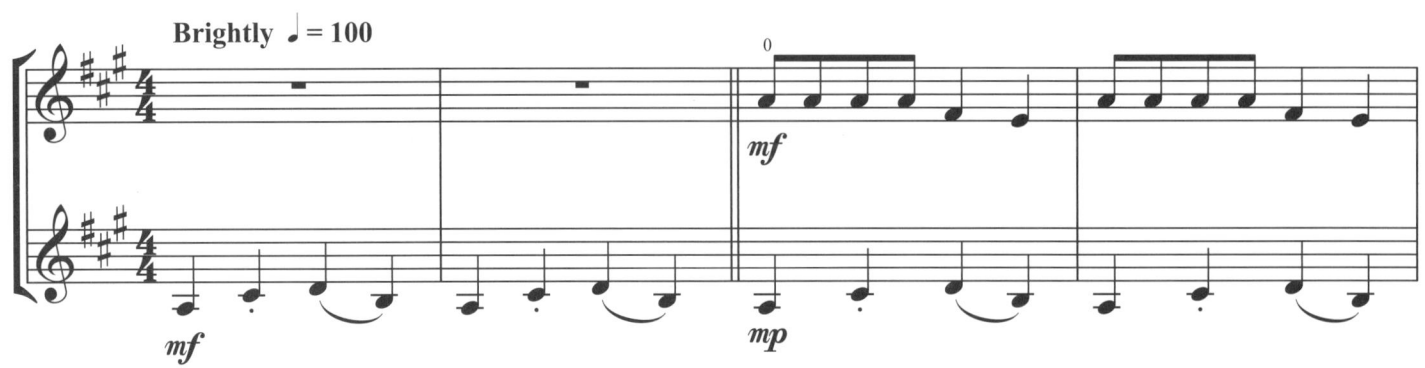

© Copyright 1988 by Boosey & Hawkes Music Publishers Ltd
From *Waggon Wheels for Violin* (ISMN 979-0-060-13553-8 & 979-0-060-13422-7)

# On Parade

Jeffery Wilson (b. 1957)
*arr.* Mainwaring

# Happy Go Lucky

Kathy & David Blackwell (b. 1958, b. 1961)

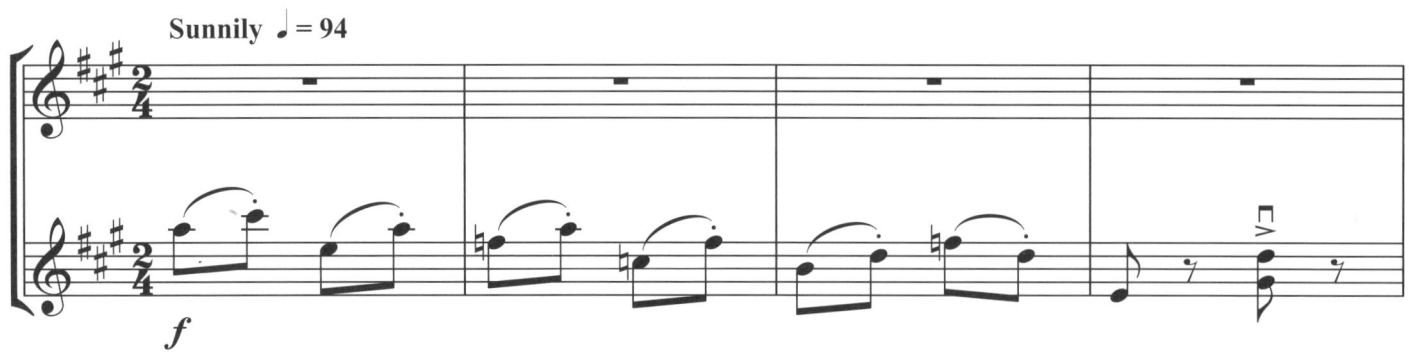

No. 30 from *Fiddle Time Joggers* by Kathy & David Blackwell © Oxford University Press 2005
This arrangement © Oxford University Press 2020. All rights reserved

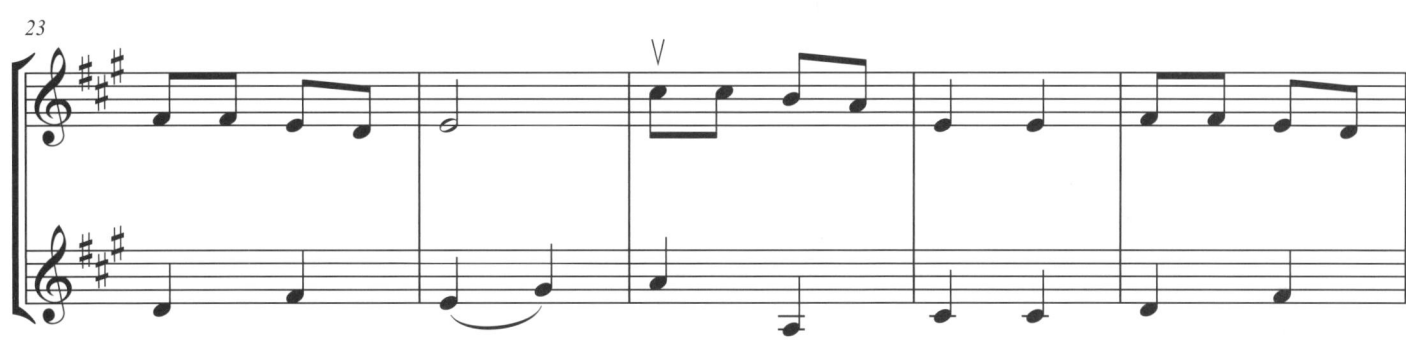
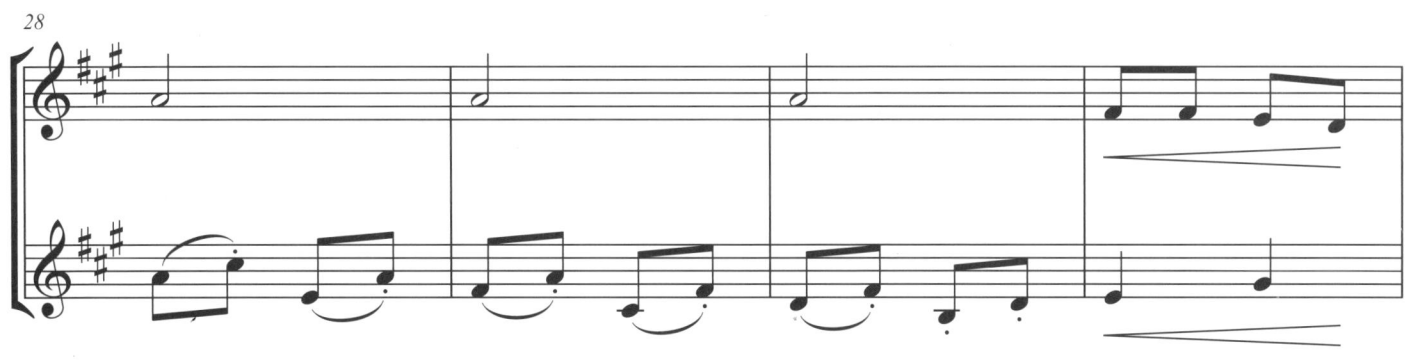

[This page has been left blank to facilitate page turns]

# Jasmine Flower

Trad., *arr.* Cobb & Yandell
Violin 2 *arr.* Mainwaring

# Pavane

Luis de Milán (ca. 1500-1561)
*arr.* Mainwaring

# The Two Roses
from *For Children, book 2*

Béla Bartók (1881-1945), *arr.* Davies
Violin 2 *arr.* Mainwaring

# Flash of Light'ning

Caroline Lumsden & Ben Attwood (b. 1951, b. 1977)
*arr.* Mainwaring

From *Wizard's Potion*, Edition Peters no. 7678 © 2003 by Peters Edition Limited, London
This arrangement © 2020 by Peters Edition Limited. All Rights Reserved. Reproduced by permission of the Publishers

# Up the Mountain

Christopher Norton (b. 1953)
*arr.* Mainwaring

# Lights Out

Jeffery Wilson (b. 1957)
*arr.* Mainwaring

[This page has been left blank to facilitate page turns]

# Air

Gottfried Finger (1660-1730)
*arr.* Mainwaring

# Menuet

adapted from *Clavierbüchlein der Anna Magdalena Bach*, BWV Anh. 114

Christian Petzold (1677-1733), *arr.* Cornick
Violin 2 *arr.* Mainwaring

From *Blue Baroque – Violin* © Copyright 2007 by Universal Edition A.G., Wien
Arrangement by Richard Mainwaring © Copyright 2020 by Universal Edition A.G., Wien

# In the Quiet House

Christopher Norton (b. 1953)
*arr.* Mainwaring

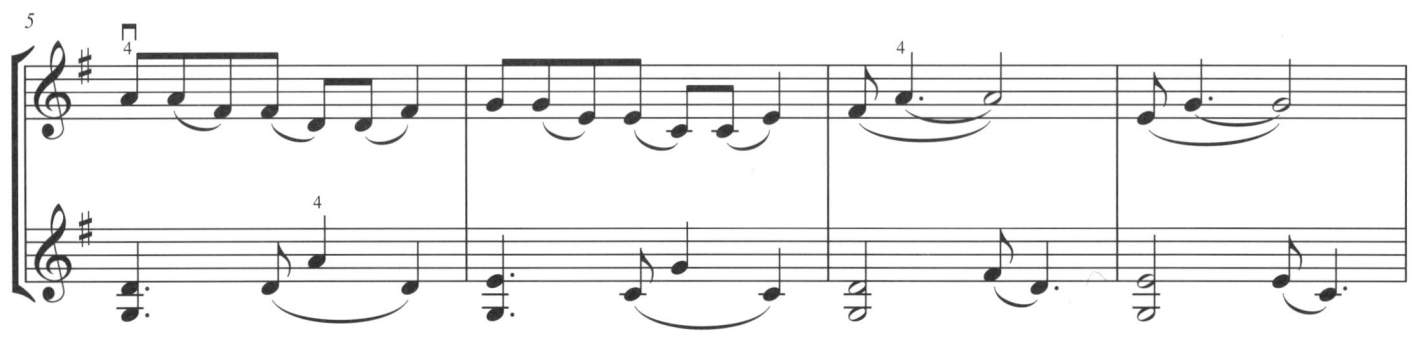
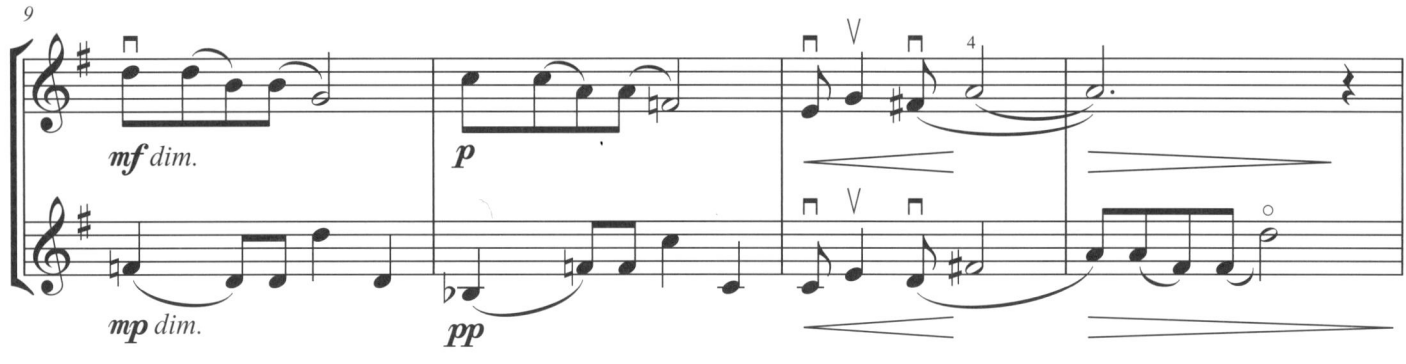

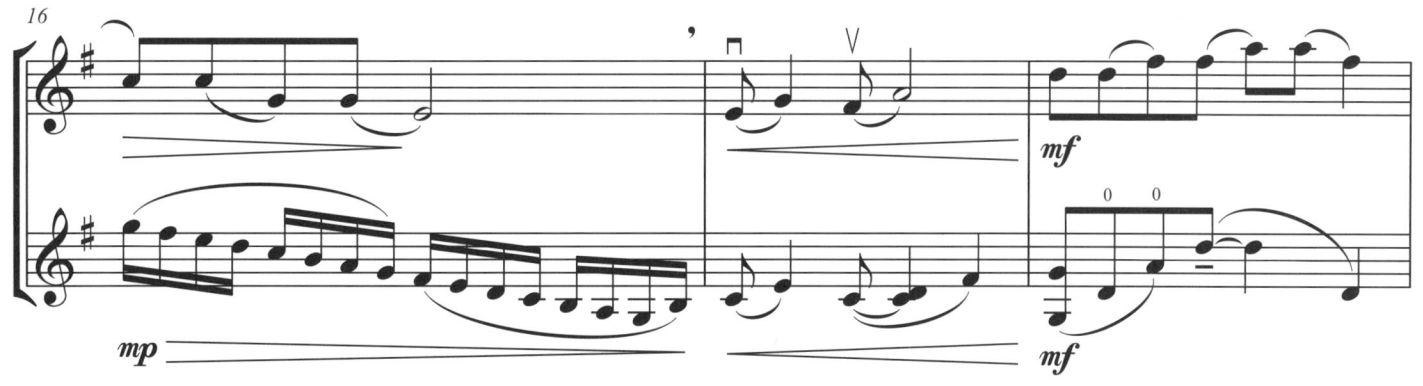

# At Work

Jeffery Wilson (b. 1957)
*arr.* Mainwaring

# Swingin' Strings

Gabriel Koeppen (b. 1958)
*arr.* Mainwaring

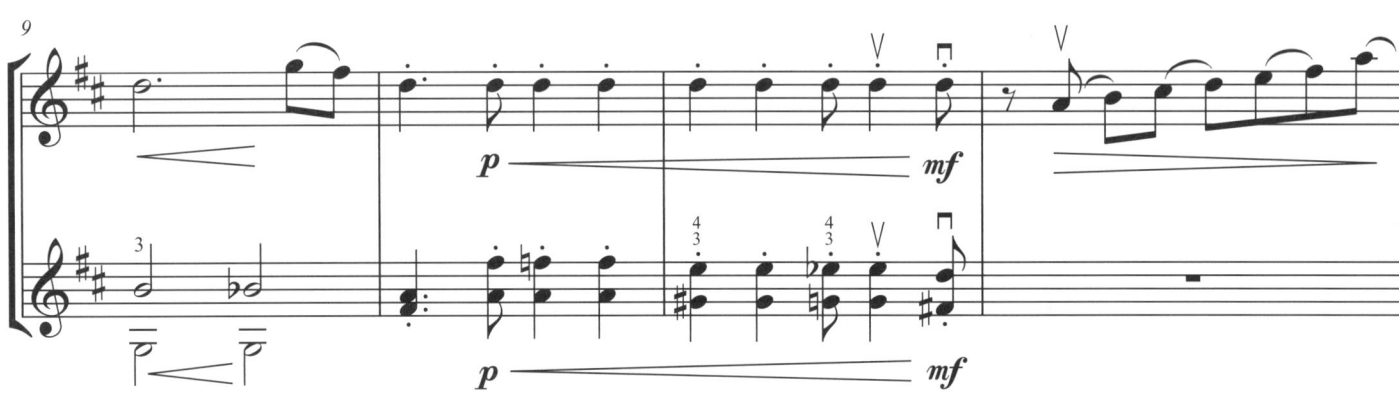

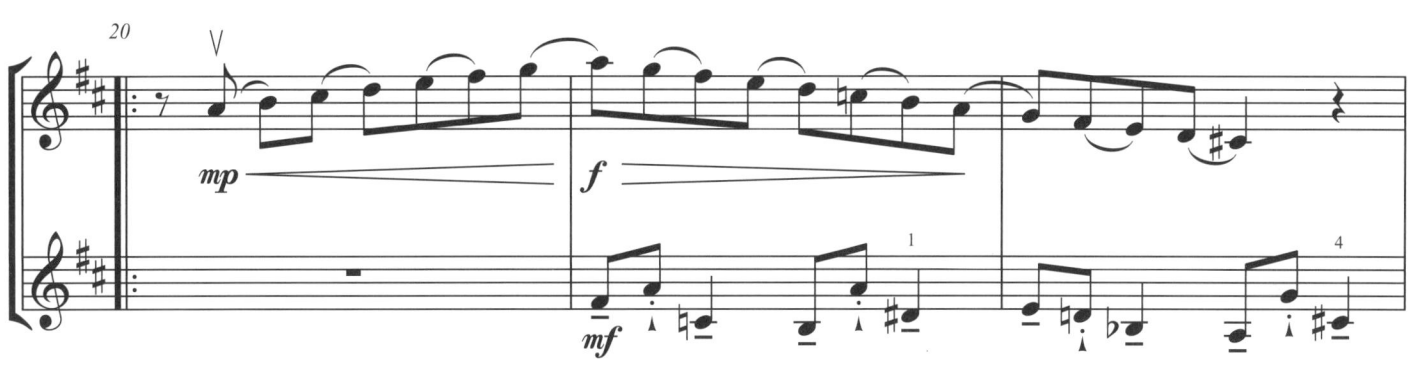

# Dublin Time

Ros Stephen (b. 1972)
*arr.* Mainwaring

From *Violin Globetrotters* © Oxford University Press 2010
This arrangement © Oxford University Press 2020. All rights reserved